FROM LEMONADE TO CORPORATE AMERICA

BUSINESS CONCEPTS FOR CHILDREN

By

GAIL SPARKS PITTS

From Lemonade to Corporate America", is a fictional story. "From Lemonade to Corporate America", introduces elementary and middle school students to business concepts through a "soap opera" type story.

A story about the life of a young girl's business journey, prepares students for the world of business through her childhood tragedies and triumphs. Although many students are not prepared to tackle the challenging industry, Vanessa's experiences take the reader through an academic yet exciting journey. The failures of many businesses are the result of misunderstanding basic concepts. "From Lemonade to Corporate America" will instill the fundamental knowledge and assist in understanding basic concepts at an early age.

As a Certified Public Accountant, who also teaches business concepts, I find that *many college students lack the knowledge critical to apply business logic. In "From Lemonade to Corporate America", the students are introduced and exposed to financial management through Vanessa's exciting life experiences.*

From Lemonade to Corporate America

Business concepts for children

Vanessa Marie was a happy child; she liked doing things that kept her busy. She enjoyed going to school - especially when she had a new pair of jeans to wear. She was in the sixth grade and was quite mischievous. She liked experiencing many different things and could not stand being bored. Her family didn't have much money, so she thought of different ways of earning money. She once made necklaces out of string to sell to her classmates; she earned very little money. One hot summer day, Vanessa decided to sell lemonade. She lived just across the street from the Boys and Girls Club where many sports activities took place. Middle school students played competitive sports there and were a bit thirsty after their games. Vanessa's lemonade sold out in a hurry. She did well.

At a sports event the following weekend, the sale of lemonade did so well that Vanessa created a business for herself. She became a *sole proprietor. A proprietor is a business owned by one person.*

She reviewed her cost and how much money she received. She thought about her cost and how much she needed to serve her customers. This is also known as the supply/demand theory. The customers want something (demand) and the business should meet the demand of the customers by supplying (providing) what the customers wanted and what would be the cost.

In order for Vanessa to have a better idea of the money she actually made after her cost, she had to make a budget. It is important for any business to know the cost in order to know how much the business can earn after the cost. If the cost is too high, compared to how much customers are willing to spend, the business will fail. So we must make a budget as illustrated below. Take a look at Vanessa's budget:

Budget for Vanessa's lemonade stand.

What is the cost one should expect?

Budget for the month of July:

Expected sales based on last week's sale of lemonade.

Sales	$300

Less Cost (expenses of items to be able to sale)

Cups (300)	$ 3
Lemonade Mix	10
Sugar	10
Ice	2
Cooler (ice chest)	20
Table rental	3
Total Cost	$ 48

Sales $300 (above)

Minus Cost $48 = $252

Sales, less cost, is known as *profit.* The above amount of $252 is Vanessa's estimated net profit. A business makes estimates because it is not likely to know the exact cost or sales. Another term businesses use for sales is *revenue.* It means how much money the business earned. It is important to remember to subtract cost (that is also known as expense) from the money earned. It is also essential to know the cost before entering into a business. As Vanessa sold more and more lemonade, she figured out different ways to make even more money based on the experience she gained as a proprietor.

The Partnership

Vanessa's lemonade sales were growing and growing. There were many sports activities at the Boys and Girls Club and many people were thirsty. The demand for lemonade grew and Vanessa knew how much was needed to supply her customers. She knew to meet the demand (customer demand) she should have enough (supply) of lemonade. Others noticed the success Vanessa was having. Her success was so great, she needed help. She decided to add a classmate, Gabriel. She ended the proprietorship and created a *partnership.* A partnership is when two or more persons share cost and profits as agreed among the partners. The agreement should be in writing. This is known as a *contract.*

The partnership business was going well and sales increased because of the additional help. Others began to notice their success. As much as Vanessa loved going to the mall and buying clothes, she also believed it to be a good idea not to spend it all at the mall. Vanessa believed if she saved half and spent half she would accomplish two goals. The first goal was to help her parents who did not have to buy many clothes for her. Vanessa's younger siblings were able to have better clothes passed down to them as she grew out of the nicer clothes she purchased with her own money. Her second goal was to save her money so that, maybe one day, she could purchase a car for herself. If she would keep her savings in the bank the bank would pay her interest and her money would grow even more. Banks pay an interest rate when you have money in their bank, it is interest you earn. In six years when she was able to drive, she could perhaps buy a car.

Gabriel

Vanessa selected Gabriel as her partner because she noticed that he was very smart. She wanted a very smart business partner and she believed Gabriel to also be very trustworthy. As they conducted business, they agreed to share the money over cost (proceeds and/or profits) at the end of the summer. The end of the summer arrived and each of them earned $1,000. Gabriel could not handle the excitement. They each had an idea the earnings would be about $1,000 each by the end of the summer, but the reality after making bank deposits all summer was a dream confirmed. They were so happy. In Gabriel's excitement, he ran home to announce his summer surprise to his parents and was hit by a car.

This was a sad tragedy because he was a good basketball player and Vanessa and he became good friends over the summer, in addition to being business partners. She visited him in the hospital. Everyday after she completed her homework after school, she went to visit Gabriel at the hospital with hopes for his quick recovery. Gabriel was severely injured in the accident. His spinal cord may have been affected and may have an influence on his ability to walk. His spleen was ruptured, causing him to bleed internally. This was a very sad time for both of them, but Vanessa never gave up on her friend. Gabriel knew his condition was not improving and his days became more and more painful. He continued to encourage Vanessa to go back to doing business the next summer. He had the courage of a lion and they shared stories of their summer experience at the Boys and Girls Club as they continued to laugh and share their joy. Gabriel was finally able to drink lemonade while in the hospital. Vanessa made lemonade from home during his last days in the hospital. She withdrew money from her bank account to purchase Gabriel a special lemonade jar for his birthday and his eyes were filled with joy. He continued to encourage her to pursue a large business one day. Sadly, Gabriel died a week later.

Vanessa's life was impacted by the tragic loss of her friend and partner. She always remembered how he encouraged her and shared his business ideas at such an early age. The following spring Vanessa became aware of her popularity due to her business activity. Everyone referred to her as the “lemonade girl.” Everyone wanted to be her friend. Although Gabriel had been quiet and didn’t have many friends, the students knew Vanessa would need a replacement when summer arrived. It was very difficult for Vanessa to choose a new partner. She knew how important it was to have someone smart, trustworthy, and good behavior while making her selection. These were far more important characteristics when conducting business. After much consideration, she selected someone in her math class - Daron. Many of her friends were angry at her for making such a choice. Why didn't she choose one of her best friends, they all wondered.

Competition

Both Crystal and Marcell were her friends and wanted to share in the business. After all, they were just as smart as Vanessa and Daron and had a good sense of how to run a business. They were furious at Vanessa and decided to no longer be her friend. In fact, they decided to steal the idea and sell their own lemonade. It was still early in the summer; they were smart, and they had time to plan. They didn't much like Vanessa and

Daron. They decided they wanted to take over the market share of lemonade sales. This could be done by stealing customers away from Vanessa and Daron. They too could be successful, were their thoughts. This is known as "*competition.*" Both Crystal and Marcell thought if they sold lemonade a dime cheaper than their competitors, they could win their customers, and they did!

They took a number of Vanessa's customers and sold lemonade at

the Boys and Girls Club at 90 cents a cup. This forced Vanessa and Daron to drop
their sale price from $1.00 to 90 cents in order for them to continue to maintain a share of the market. The market is the customers. Every summer it was a continuous fight for the customer market share but all of them did very well. They all learned the secret of earning money on their money. Remember, the bank pays for the use of your money -called *interest.* They all saved to see who

would save the most and who would have the best car. Well, except Marcell - he spent all of his money at the mall. In later years, Marcell had to catch rides with Crystal because he spent all his money on taking trips and buying fancy clothes.

A few years later, while they were all in their senior year of high school, to the surprise of all of them, some college kids noticed the demand of customers wanting to buy drinks during a sports activity. The college students got jobs and saved their money to purchase vending machines and put all the kids out of business by taking over the market at the Boys and Girls Club.

The availability of cold drinks in the vending machines offered more choices for customers and they received more for their money. All the kids previously in business lost all of their customers. This saddened Vanessa and Daron, as well as

Crystal and Marcell. They decided to come together and become friends. All four grew up, finished high school and became close friends. They all attended Michigan State University (MSU) in East Lansing, Michigan. Despite the many distractions of college life and friends who are not as committed to success, the four of them remained focused. Vanessa would always reflect and remember Gabriel. She encouraged the other three friends to stay focused by reminding them that hard work, studying, commitment and compassion would result in success one day. She encouraged them as Gabriel encouraged her.

The Business Returns

Vanessa and her three friends selected “Business" as their major at MSU. They learned business to help them succeed and to prevent others from coming and taking their customers. They learned the hard way, and Vanessa never forgot the pain of losing Gabriel. She remembered what he taught her. They learned not to allow someone to take away their business. After a lot of research and sharing of ideas, they decided to form a *corporation.* A corporation is a business approved by the state to allow persons to conduct business in a fictitious (made up) name and the business may sell stock to earn money from persons willing to invest in the business. Their corporation was "Gabriel, Inc."

The group decided who would be the best in each part of the business. Vanessa was responsible for marketing and advertising. It was her job to get the word out about the business and tell how their company could meet the needs of their customers at a low cost. Marcell was good at sales; he had a way of making people feel they really needed his product. Daron was best at keeping track of the money and made sure the cost was low and the business would only spend money when necessary. Crystal took care of the legal part of the business and had great people skills that allowed her to work well with others. With their combined skills, also known as *teamwork*, they decided to develop and sell used furniture, records and appliances near campus.

They knew this was a great idea because college students did not want to pay a lot of money for anything. They decided to sell shares of the stock to the public to increase the worth of the business. They were attracting investors and had filed all the necessary papers with the State of Michigan, where they conducted their business. They also filed the required documents with the Security Exchange Commission (SEC) to protect the new investors. The SEC is a federal agency created to provide trust to people who invest their money in a company. Investors buy stock with hopes of making money. Companies pay some of their profits (sales minus cost) to their investors and this is known as a *dividend* payment. This is to encourage more and more investors.

The company was very successful. Customers purchased used items and returned furniture after graduating. The furniture was resold. They paid very little to get the furniture returned. With their business ideas, and experience in their early years, they decided to expand and make the business bigger, so no one could take over their market share. They decided to rent furniture, get furniture at garage sales, auctions, and places going out of business. They marked up their cost to customers to make money. They would mark up items just enough to make a certain profit. They decided in advance how much money was needed, and this determined the sale price while keeping in mind what students could afford and were willing to pay.

They had a budget, sold stock and paid dividends. This is how good businesses grow. People go into business to make money; this would allow the business to remain in existence. This is known as a "*going concern.*" The business did extremely well and they all continued to make money.

Drama

As the following school year began, business was at its peak. Vanessa enjoyed her partners and their success. Their experience and hard work was paying off; they were very successful. They had profits beyond their belief. Gabriel, Inc. was making so much money, they moved to a larger building to accommodate the demand of their ever growing customers. The larger building was four times the size of the old store. Life was good and Vanessa knew Gabriel would be pleased. As she continued to think of Gabriel, she remembered him saying, "work hard -- success is not easy. Failure is easy; don't ever give up on your dream."

There were days when it was hard because sometimes Vanessa saw things differently from Crystal, Marcell and Daron. They were all equal and when disagreements occurred, they had to vote. The vote was based on what the

majority of them wanted to do. Since Vanessa had a good business mind, she was still learning to improve herself and become a better business woman. Gabriel would say, "The biggest room in the house is the room for improvement. As you strive to improve -- never lose
sight of what is important, don't let the small things get you down and when you get down, pick yourself back up and find another road. There are many roads to

success and you just have to find the right path."

Winter arrived; the campus was snow covered and cold. Not much was going on since it was so cold. Most students chose to stay in their warm dormitory rooms after attending their classes. It was more quiet than normal and Daron wanted to do something to fight the winter blues. He decided to seek out something new and different. He ventured out to a different side of town. He was not familiar with the area but he knew it to be a safe area. He decided to stop and shop at a shopping mall about 20 miles away. He spent and spent and spent. He enjoyed looking good and buying new things. He was the only one of the group who bragged of his success and showed off his *assets.* Assets are items that you own. He met a beautiful young lady, Carmen, while at the mall. Although she did not attend college, he was taken by her beauty.

Love, Friendship and Business

Carmen and Daron spent a lot of time together over their first week of meeting. It was love at first sight. Daron was quick to jump into things without taking time to think more of what he was doing. He was often led by how things looked. As the weeks passed, they spent more time together. Daron was a serious student and hard worker. He kept up his grades and continued to work hard for Gabriel, Inc.

Daron bought small gifts for Carmen. She began asking him for small amounts of money. He had plenty of it, so this was not a problem for him. The amounts of money needed by Carmen became large and more frequent. She gave him a story about a family illness. Daron had no idea; Carmen spotted him driving up to the mall in his new BMW. She followed him and took notice of his spending. She was aware of her beauty and sought out young and old men with money.

About two months had passed and their relationship continued to grow. Carmen began to increase the amount of money from Daron to much larger and larger amounts than before. As Daron was very busy with school and work, he had no idea Carmen was using drugs. He was too busy to notice the signs. She hid the signs well. Drugs were beginning to take a toll on her appearance, but Daron was far too in love with her at this point to even notice there was something wrong. He used all of his savings to help Carmen for whatever she needed. She was a druggie and did anything for drugs, including lying about her family needing money. She lied, she cheated and she was a thief. Daron only saw certain things.

As time passed, Daron began stealing money from the business to help Carmen. He had the ability to buy items for the business and use the business money. He was the only one responsible for paying for items for the business.

A good business should not be destroyed by friendship or love, Daron learned. This was a lesson for Crystal, Marcell and Vanessa as well. They forgot about the importance of staying on top of the business. Since they had a lot of money they thought that was all they needed. They were successful.

They did not know about the importance of watching the money. Vanessa was crushed. This went on for a few weeks. Daron was clever; he hid his stealing from the business from the others. Vanessa realized she should not have allowed the business to have only one person in charge of buying and paying for items. It is important to separate what each person does and then check to make sure things are working as they should. This is known as internal *control.*

This painful lesson put Gabriel, Inc. out of business. They lost everything in the business but later became friends again. They all completed college. They all learned about saving money, trust, not to be careless in money and how to apply business concepts. They all became very successful and did well in life. Vanessa became a business school teacher, Crystal a corporate spokesperson, Marcell a project manager and Daron a school teacher like Vanessa.

Quiz

1. What is a partnership?
2. What is a corporation?
3. What is revenue?
4. What is an expense?
5. What is supply?
6. What is demand?
7. What is interest rate?
8. What is a going concern?
9. What is a budget?
10. What is a contract?
11. What is the Security Exchange Commission?
12. What is a dividend?
13. What is a profit?

You did it!

Welcome to the world of business!

www.ingramcontent.com/pod-product-compliance
Lightning Source LLC
LaVergne TN
LVHW052031170826
845678LV00019B/2546

* 9 7 9 8 8 3 9 6 9 0 4 8 6 *